THE MALIGN MISCHIEF OF
MEGABITE

STEVE BARLOW - STEVE SKIDMORE
ILLUSTRATED BY PIPI SPOSITO

Franklin Watts
First published in Great Britain in 2020
by The Watts Publishing Group

Text © Steve Barlow and Steve Skidmore 2020
Illustrations © Franklin Watts 2020
Cover design: Cathryn Gilbert

ISBN 978 1 4451 7012 1
ebook ISBN 978 1 4451 7014 5
Library ebook ISBN 978 1 4451 7013 8

1 3 5 7 9 10 8 6 4 2

Printed in Great Britain

Franklin Watts
An imprint of
Hachette Children's Group
Part of The Watts Publishing Group
Carmelite House
50 Victoria Embankment
London EC4Y 0DZ

An Hachette UK Company
www.hachette.co.uk

www.franklinwatts.co.uk

HOW TO BE A MEGAHERO

Some superheroes can read books with their X-ray vision without opening the covers or even when they're in a different room ...

Others can read them while flying through the air or stopping a runaway train.

But that stuff *IS* just small potatoes to you, because you're not a superhero. You're a *MEGAHERO*!

YES, this book is about **YOU**! And you don't just read it to the end and then stop. You read a bit: then you make a choice that takes you to a different part of the book. You might jump from Section 3 to 47 or 28!

If you make a good choice, *GREAT!*

BUUUUUUT ...

If you make the wrong choice ... **DA-DA-DAAAH!**

ALL KINDS OF BAD STUFF WILL HAPPEN.

Too bad! It's no good turning green and tearing your shirt off. You'll just have to start again. But that won't happen, will it?

Because you're not a zero, or even a superhero. You are ... *MEGAHERO*!

You are a **BRILLIANT INVENTOR** — but one day **THE SUPER PARTICLE-ACCELERATING COSMIC RAY COLLIDER** you'd made out of old drinks cans, lawnmower parts and a mini black hole went critical and scrambled your molecules (nasty!). When you finally stopped screaming, smoking and bouncing off the walls, you found your body had changed! Now you can transform into any person, creature or object. *How awesome is that?!!!*

You communicate with your *MEGACOMPUTER* companion, **PAL**, through your *MEGASHADES* sunglasses (which make you look pretty COOL, too). **PAL** controls the things you turn into and *almost hardly ever crashes and has to be turned off and on again!* This works perfectly — unless you have a bad WIFI signal, or **PAL** gets something wrong — but hey! That's computers for you, right?

Like all heroes, your job is to SAVE THE WORLD from **BADDIES AND THEIR EVIL SCHEMES**. But be back in time for supper. Even *MEGAHEROES* have to eat …

Go to 1.

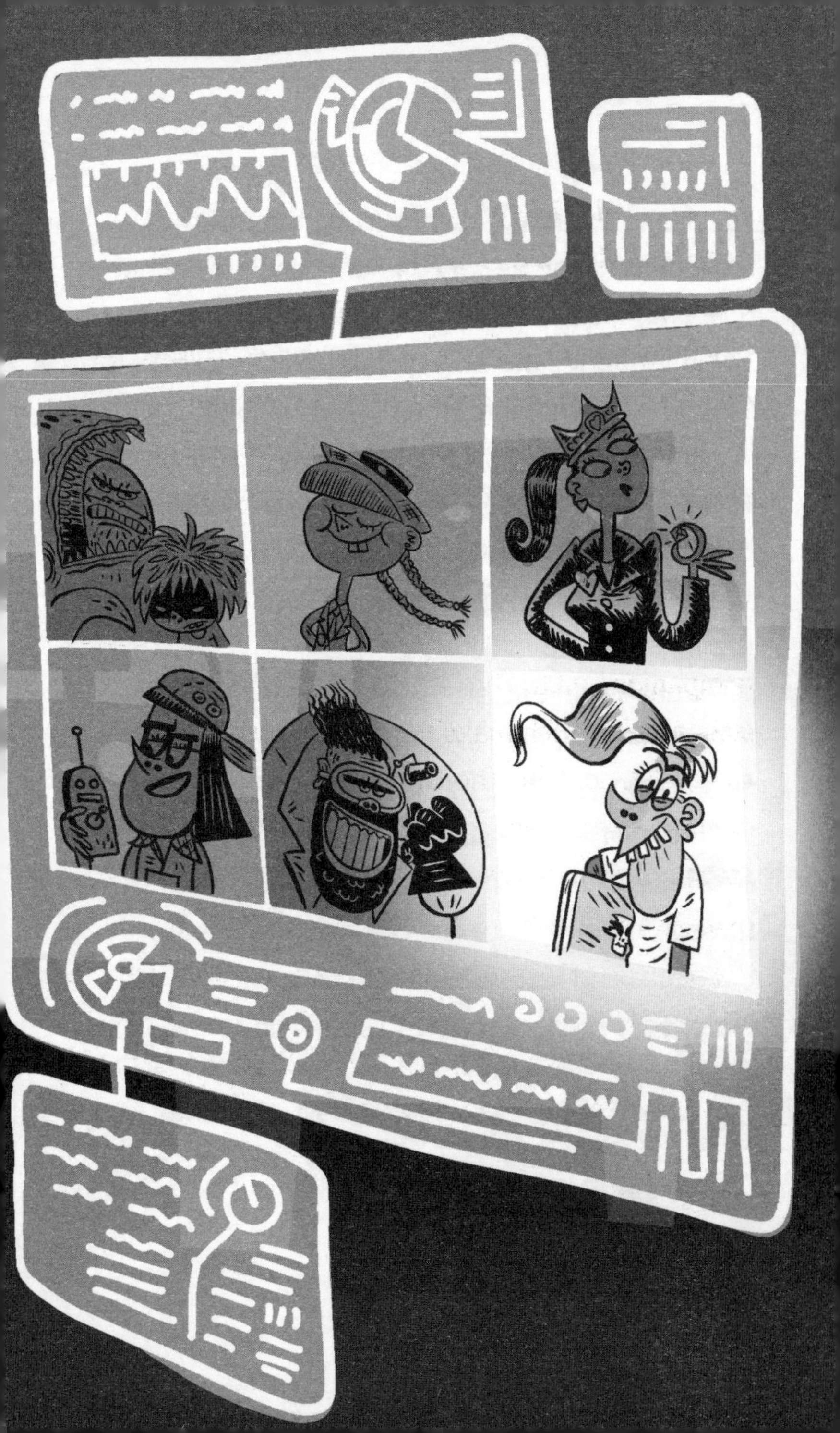

You are in the **MEGA** cave, surfing the Internet, looking for some new **MEGA** hero costume supplies on *PantsForMegaHeroes.net.*

"What about the blue underpants?" you ask PAL. "I'd look good in those!" You hit **BUY.**

"NOT REALLY YOUR COLOUR!" says PAL. "HOW ABOUT BROWN, THEN IT WON'T SHOW ANY … **WHAAARGHHHHHH! FIZZ! FLIPPITY FIZZ! BUZZ, ZOINK!**"

The **MEGA** cave lights up as PAL's circuits begin fizzing and popping!

"What's the matter?" you ask.

"SECURITY SYSTEMS BREACHED," gasps PAL. "SOMETHING'S GOT INTO MY SYSTEM!"

"But that's impossible," you say. "You have **MEGA** firewalls! Nothing should be able to get through them!"

Flames and smoke begin to shoot out of PAL's circuits. "I THINK THAT MIGHT BE A WRONG ASSUMPTION! **HELP!**"

To reboot PAL, go to 14.

To try and put the fire out, go to 38.

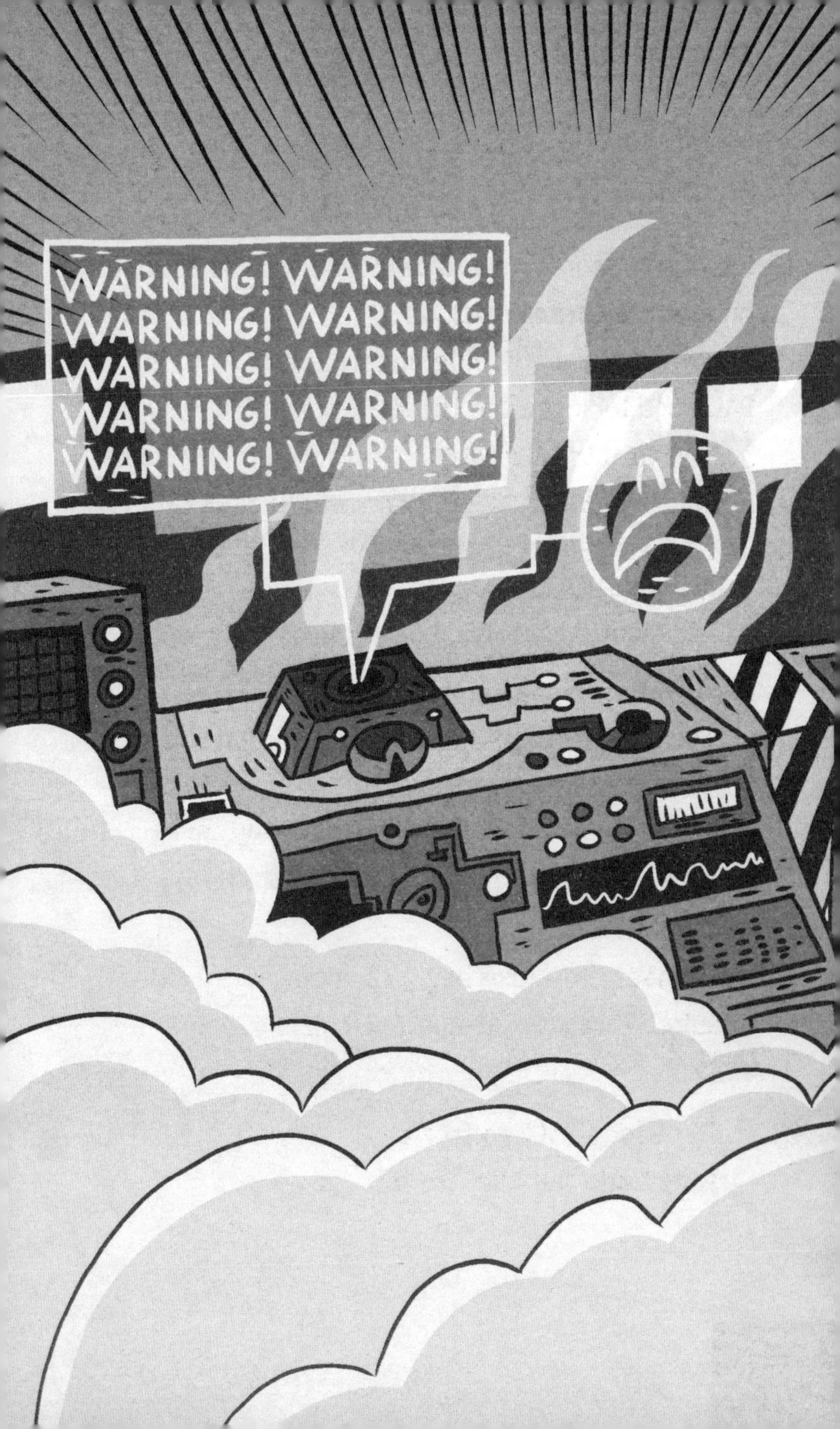
WARNING! WARNING!
WARNING! WARNING!
WARNING! WARNING!
WARNING! WARNING!
WARNING! WARNING!

2

You hit **COMMAND** and *MEGABITE* appears in the *MEGA* cave as a 3D hologram, floating in CYBERSPACE.

"Curse you, *MEGAHERO!*" he growls.

"I have total command over you," you tell *MEGABITE*. "You're trapped and only I can set you free. **BUT** you've got to promise not to do any more *MEGA* bad stuff, otherwise you're staying where you are ..."

"All right, I promise," he replies. "All I wanted to do was take over the world ..."

"You're just more **BARK** than **BITE**!" you tell *MEGABITE*. "OK, PAL, let him out, but stick him in quarantine, where Internet nasties belong!"

Go to 50.

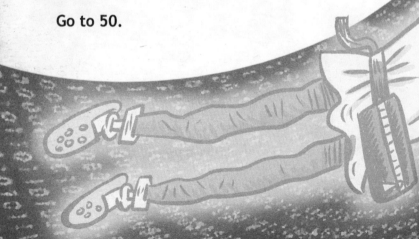

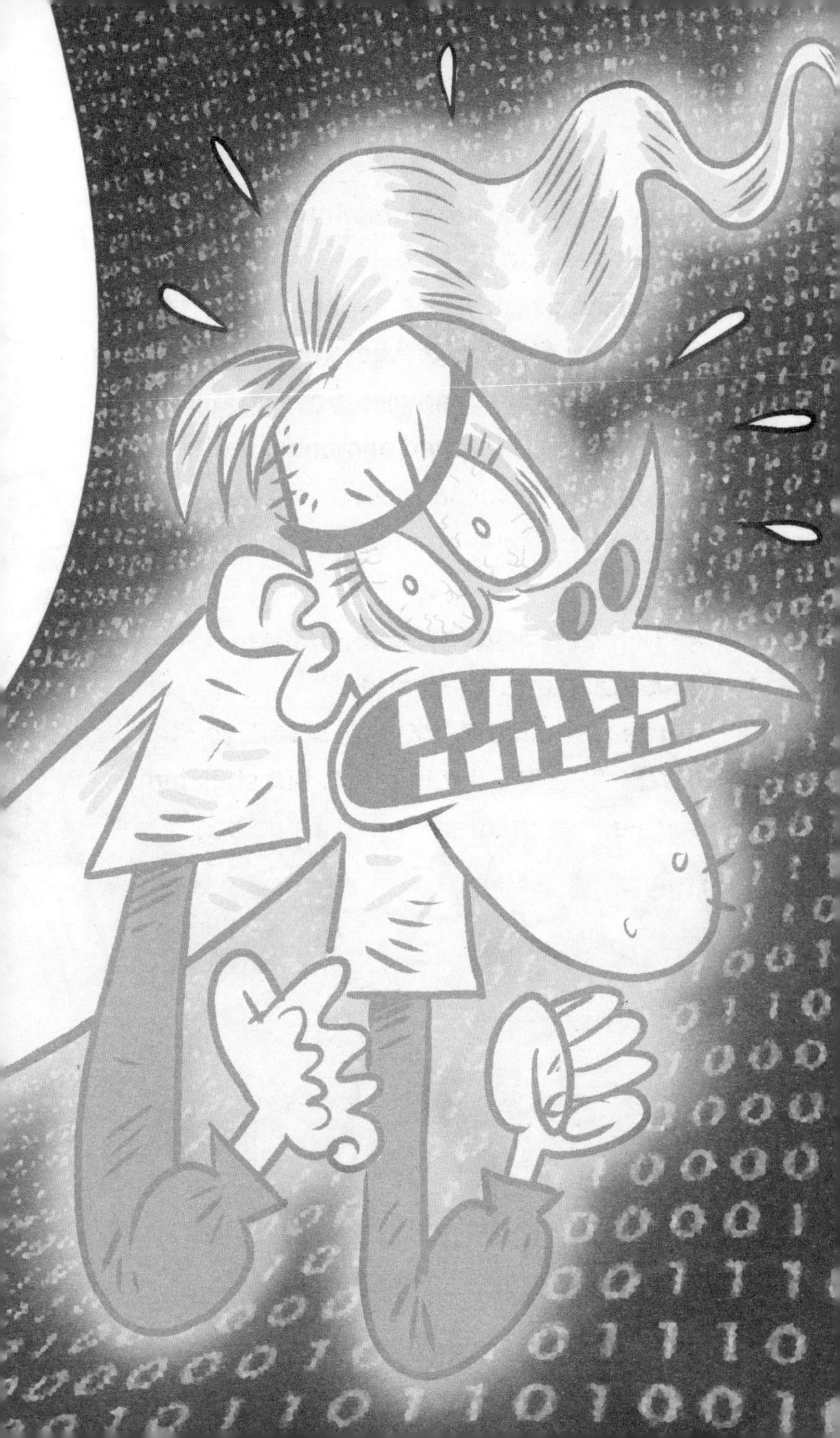

3

"Send me to the hacker through the network," you say.

"THAT'S NOT GOING TO WORK," replies PAL. "THE HACKER IS CHANGING ROUTES EVERY SECOND AND PUTTING UP FIREWALLS. YOU COULD BE LOST IN CYBERSPACE FOREVER. YOU'LL HAVE TO GET THERE IN PERSON."

Go to 28.

4

You search PAL's **MEGA VILLAIN** database but find nothing ...

We're going to have to do something else ... you think.

Go to 20.

5

You keep pulling, but **MEGABITE** is too strong for your tongue!

Bit by bit he prises it from the computer until he holds your froggy tongue in his hand.

"Geg go og gy tongue," you say.

"Let go of your tongue? Certainly!" **MEGABITE** releases his grip and the tongue snaps back into your face, sending you hurtling through the air.

"It's a flying frog," he laughs.

"Right, **MEGABITE**, I'm hopping mad with you! The froggy fun is over! Turn me back into human form," you tell PAL. The computer obeys.

Go to 49.

6

You turn back into human form. "OK, kid," you say. "I don't know why you did what you did, but this is the end of the road for you. I'm taking you in ..."

The teenager smiles. "Firstly, I'm not a kid, I am **MEGABITE**! And secondly ... no you're not!"

Go to 49.

"I'll run a check on you and try to discover what caused all this **MEGA** bad stuff," you tell PAL. "Turn me into an antivirus."

"I'LL TRY MY BEST. MY HARDWARE SEEMS TO HAVE GONE ALL FLOPPY."

There is a long pause. "Why have you changed me into an old lady and not an antivirus?" you ask.

"SORRY, MY SYSTEMS THOUGHT YOU SAID, **'AN AUNTY IRIS'**." PAL turns you back into human form. "YOU DID LOOK SWEET THOUGH!"

"I don't care what I looked like," you say. "We need to find out what's got into you and stop it before it fries you again."

"OK, KEEP YOUR **MEGA** PANTS ON! I KNOW WHAT TO DO," replies PAL.

To find out what PAL's idea is, go to 26.

8

"We're gonna need a bigger boat," you tell PAL.

MEGABITE opens his jaws but before he can clamp down on you, PAL transforms you into a Naval Patrol Boat.

CLANG!

MEGABITE's teeth shatter against your metal hull.

"I bet that *MEGABITE* hurt," you laugh.

As *MEGABITE* swims away, you aim your guns at him.

To open fire, go to 27.

To ask him to surrender, go to 41.

9

"Let's track the hack!" you say. Zooming through cyberspace, you follow the route the **BUGS** and **VIRUSES** came from.

Seconds later you come to a stop. "SOURCE FOUND!" reports PAL.

"OK, get me out of the cyber world and send me to the hacker's location!"

PAL sends an escape command through cyberspace and turns you back into human form.

"**AARGGHHH!**" you scream.

"WHAT ON EARTH IS THE PROBLEM?" asks PAL.

"I'm not on Earth!" you reply. "That's the problem! I'm hanging onto a satellite **ABOVE** the **EARTH**! And I'm running out of breath!"

To turn back into a bug, go to 36.
To turn into a spaceship, go to 47.

"I need to follow him," you tell PAL. "Get me into his system!"

Instantly you are back inside the cyber world as a **TRACKER COOKIE**, following *MEGABITE*. You head through thousands of networks, but can't locate him.

"Where is he?" you ask.

"HE'S HIDDEN HIMSELF," replies PAL. "MY GUESS IS HE'S HEADED INTO A VIRTUAL REALITY WORLD OR THE SHADOW WEB."

To explore the Shadow web, go to 25.

To explore a virtual reality world, go to 37.

11

"Open up the firewall for a millisecond and I'll sneak through," you tell PAL.

"HAVE YOU GONE **MEGA** CRAZY!" says PAL. "THAT WILL LET THE **BUGS** AND **VIRUSES** INTO MY SYSTEM AGAIN! WE NEED TO DESTROY THEM FIRST!"

To take PAL's advice, go to 23.

To ignore PAL's advice, go to 17.

12

"And how do you think you'll achieve **TOTAL WORLD DOMINATION?**" you ask, playing for time.

"I will control the cyber world through my army of Internet **BUGS AND VIRUSES** and my *MEGABOTS*! Everyone will have to do what I say and give me what I want. **EVERYTHING** will be in my power — banks, companies, governments — **EVERYTHING** and **EVERYONE**! I just needed to get rid of you and PAL and now I have!"

"Well, that's not quite true ..." you say.

To grab *MEGABITE*, go to 49.

To grab *MEGABITE*'s computer, go to 19.

13

One of **MEGABITE**'s tentacles crashes down
towards you.

"MOVE TO YOUR LEFT!" says PAL.

You do and the tentacle hits the **ESCAPE** key.

The virtual world instantly disappears. You
hurtle through a collapsing cyber world. Lines
of code and data stream past you. Then there
is a roaring noise, a flash of light and you find
yourself back in the **MEGA** cave.

"That was a **MEGA** idea," you say. "Now we
need to make sure **MEGABITE** is stopped once and
for all!"

To hit the DELETE key, go to 35.

To hit the COMMAND key, go to 2.

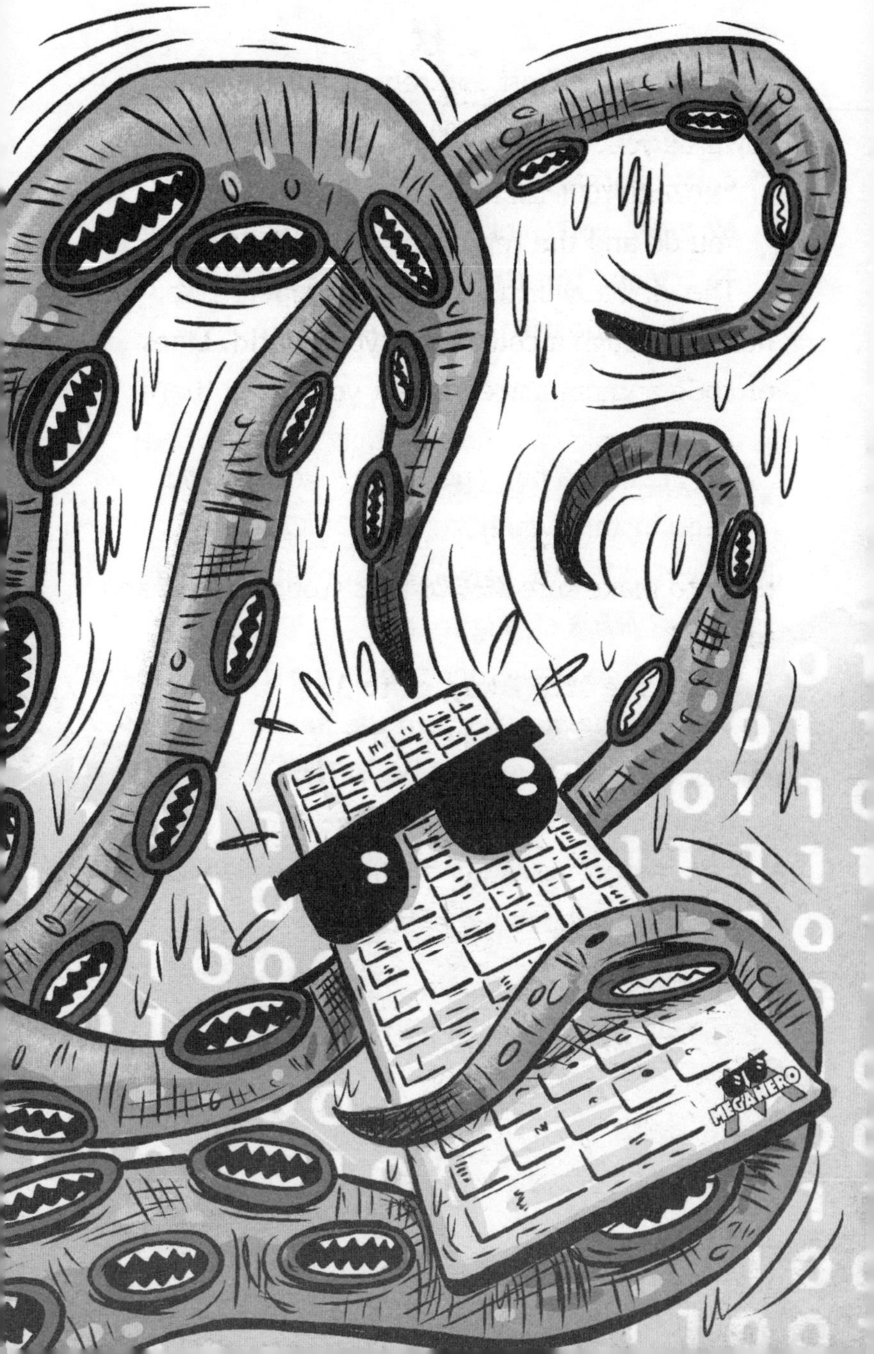
MEGANERO

14

"Switch yourself off and reboot," you say.

"SQUAWK! WIBBLE! BER-DONG!" replies PAL, as its circuits continue to fizz and fry.

Hmmm, you think. That's not going to work ...

To try and put the fire out, go to 38.

To disconnect PAL, go to 43.

15

"Turn me into a hippopotamus," you tell PAL.

In an instant you become a **2000 KILOGRAM** grey battering ram with a huge mouth of **MEGA** strong teeth!

You charge at the door, reducing it to splinters as you smash your way into the flat. It is full of **HI-TECH** computer **GIZMO STUFF!**

A teenager sits at a desk in front of a laptop. "Hello, hippo, or rather should I say, **MEGAHERO?**" he says. "I've been expecting you!"

To arrest the teenager, go to 6.

To talk to him, go to 22.

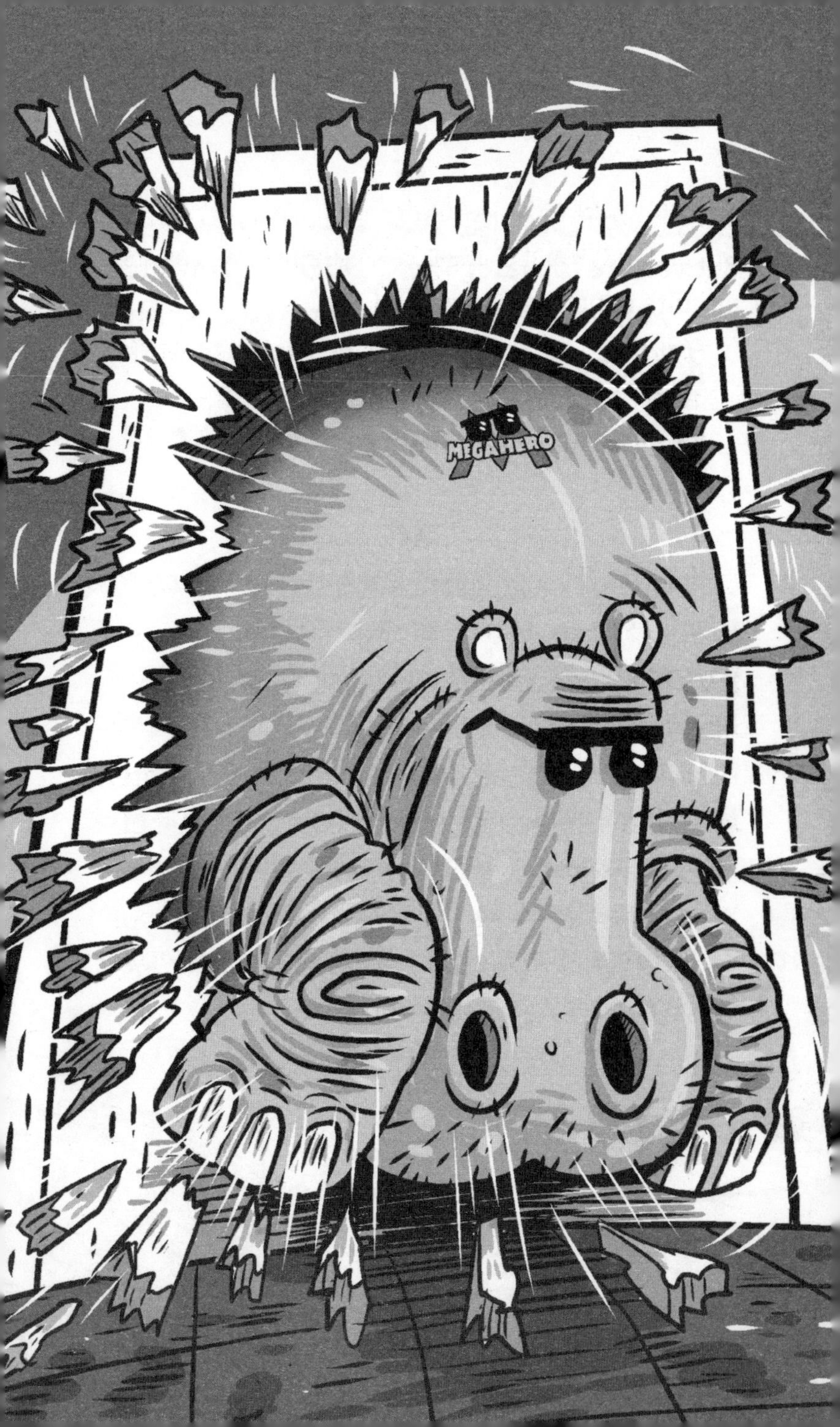

16

"Get me out of here, PAL!" you order.

But you are too late. The **C-BUGS** swarm all over you, nibbling on your sweet cookie dough!

DA-DA-DAAAH!

CRUMBS! That wasn't good. ***GO BACK TO 1***.

17

"That will let the hacker know that we're on to them," you explain. "We need to be clever. Set your system to upload and reverse the flow of data. When I'm in place, switch off the firewall, for a millisecond, so I can sneak through. Then turn the firewall back on before any bugs can get into our system. The hacker won't know what we've done and I can hunt them down!"

"HMMM. MAYBE THAT WILL WORK AND MAYBE YOU'RE NOT SO **MEGA** CRAZY AFTER ALL," says PAL.

You smile. "No, I'm ***MEGA CLEVA!***"

Go to 40.

18

"Turn me into a bird so I can fly away, **NOW!**"

PAL obeys and you change into a gull. However, as you soar up, **MEGABITE**, in shark form, leaps from the water. The shark's jaws open and snap shut, trapping you.

"**OUCH!**" you squawk.

You try to break free, but it is hopeless. **MEGABITE** has bitten! You are dragged back into the water.

DA-DA-DAAAH!

You're not going to be shaking your tail feathers any more! *Go back to 1.*

"Turn me into a giant long-tongued frog," you whisper. PAL obeys.

You shoot out your tongue, which sticks to the computer. You begin to pull it towards you.

MEGABITE gives a cry and grabs hold of the computer. You're in a tug of war!

To change into something else, go to 44.
To keep your froggy form, go to 5.

"We need to set a trap for the hacker," you say. "Turn me into a tracker bug and put me inside the cyber networks. Then we go back onto the *PantsForMegaHeroes* site and when the hacker tries to get into your system, we reverse everything, get into theirs and I can track them down!"

"THAT'S A **MEGA** PLAN!" says PAL.

"That's why I'm a *MEGAHERO*!" you reply modestly. "Turn me into a bug."

You become a six-foot insect!

"How is a giant bug going to get inside a computer network?" you ask PAL. "I meant an ELECTRONIC bug!"

"OOPS, SORRY ..."

There's a flash of light and you find yourself in cyberspace.

To set up a firewall barrier, go to 45.

To open up the *PantsForMegaHeroes* site, go to 30.

"Turn me into a **BUG** killer!" you order.

You turn into a giant fly swatter. "I was thinking more of a bug spray," you say, "but that'll do!"

You swat at the bugs, squashing their mechanical parts, until there are none left.

You turn back into human form. "*MEGABITE* isn't here. I need to get off this island, PAL."

To head into the Shadow web, go to 25.
To turn into a boat, 31.
To fly off the island, 39.

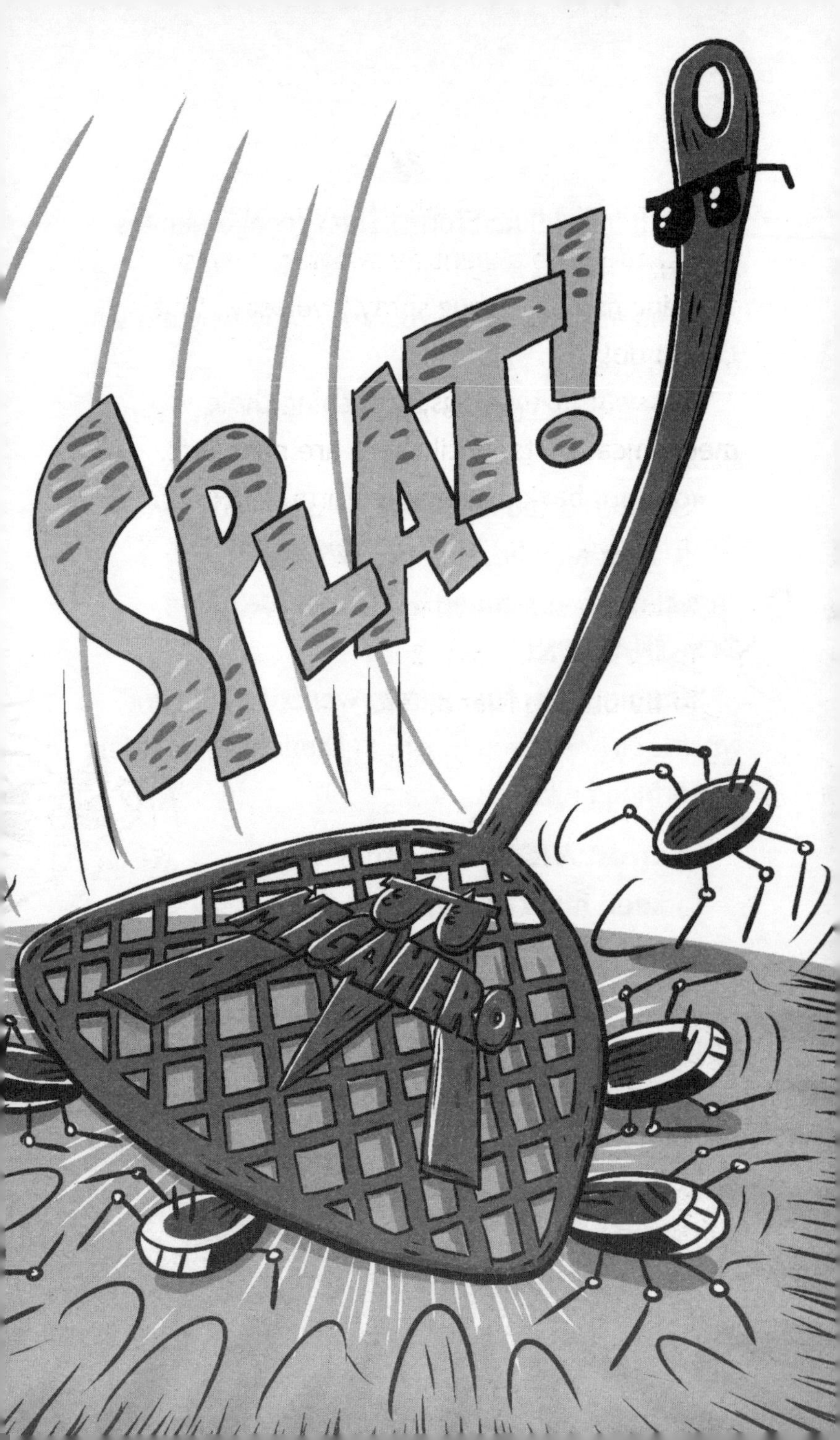
SPLAT!

22

You turn into human form. The teenager smiles at you.

"Who are you, kid?" you ask. "And why did you try and destroy PAL?"

"I'm not a **KID**!" replies the teenager. "I'm **MEGABITE**!"

"OK, kid called **MEGABITE**, what's your game?"

"It's not a game," replies **MEGABITE**. "It's serious. It's called **TOTAL WORLD DOMINATION**!"

"Oh, not the usual *villain-wants-to-rule-the-world routine*!" you laugh. "I thought it would be something new!"

To arrest **MEGABITE**, go to 49.

To keep him talking, go to 12.

23

"Zap all **BUGS** and **VIRUSES**!" you order.

"Here goes!" PAL sends an electronic surge through its systems. As it pulses through, zapping everything buggy, you suddenly realise something important!

YOU ARE A BUG!

"PAL stop the ..."

DA-DA-DAAAH!

Too late — you've been *zapped*! Go back to 1.

24

"Turn me into something that can get under the door," you tell PAL.

PAL transforms you into a puddle of water. You ooze under the door.

ZAPPPPPPPPPP!

An electric shock hits you! The door was booby-trapped! You begin to turn into steam ...

DA-DA-DAAAH!

Water and electricity don't mix! Go back to 1.

25

"OK, then I'm heading into the Shadow web," you say.

"NO, THAT'S A BAD IDEA ..."

But PAL's warning is too late. As you enter the **SHADOW WEB**, everything goes black! You have no idea where you are or where you're going!

"PAL! Get me out of here ..."

There's no reply. In the Shadow web everything is hidden. You're stuck in the shadows.

DA-DA-DAAAH!

The clue was in the name! Go back to 1.

"So, what should we do?" you ask.

"I'LL RUN A CHECK ON WHY I WENT FIZZ," replies PAL.

"Make it quick, we don't want another attack on you. The next one could be **DEADLY**! And without you, there'd be no **MEGAHERO**."

"THANKS FOR YOUR CONCERN," replies PAL.

Seconds later the computer reports back. "WHEN YOU HIT BUY ON **PANTSFORMEGAHEROES.NET**, MILLIONS OF **BUGS** AND **VIRUSES** HACKED INTO THE **MEGA** CYBER SYSTEM AND OVERLOADED ME. THAT'S WHY THEY GOT THROUGH MY FIREWALL!"

"Who do you think is behind this dastardly attack?" you ask.

"SOMEONE WHO HAS **MEGA** HACKING SKILLS AND WANTS TO DESTROY YOUR POWERS," replies PAL.

You nod. "Well I've got to admit, there's lots of **MEGAVILLAINS** out there who want to get rid of us."

To make sure PAL has got rid of all the bugs and viruses, go to 48.

To search your MEGA villain database for the hacker, go to 34.

27

You open fire, but **MEGABITE** simply disappears and the shells explode harmlessly in the water.

"Where did he go?" you ask PAL.

"I'm behind you!"

You look and see **MEGABITE** has turned into a **MEGA BATTLESHIP**. His guns are trained on you.

"I told you, I can be anything in my virtual world!" he laughs. "I'm **MEGA SORRY** but it's bye-bye time! Open fire!"

DA-DA-DAAAH!

Actually, it's **BOOM** time! Go back to 1.

28

"OK, turn me into a spaceship."

PAL obeys and soon you are re-entering Earth's atmosphere, heading for London.

BOOM!

The air around turns into a fiery ball of red and yellow.

"I'm being attacked!" you cry.

"I HAD NOTICED!" replies PAL. "THE EXPLOSIONS WERE A GIVEAWAY."

You are rocked sideways as more explosions fill the air.

"INCOMING!" warns PAL.

Dozens of fighter jets are heading towards you firing missiles!

"Why are they attacking?" you ask.

"I'm listening to the pilot's COMMS," reports PAL. "They think you're an alien UFO!"

To tell the pilots who you are, go to 32.

To change into something else, go to 42.

"Turn me into a **MEGA** hammer," you tell PAL.

PAL obeys and you smash down onto **MEGABITE**'s equipment.

ZAPPPPP!

Thousands of volts of electricity surge through your **STEEL BODY!**

MEGABITE booby-trapped the equipment! Your shades are fried and you can't connect to PAL. Changing form on your own would need serious thought — and serious thinking is something a hammer isn't good at! You are stuck in this form forever!

DA-DA-DAAAH!

That wasn't such a smashing time!
Go back to 1.

"Open up the *PantsForMegaHeroes* site," you tell PAL. The computer obeys.

Suddenly PAL's system is attacked by millions of **BUGS** and **VIRUSES**. They swarm all over you!

"Get me out!" you tell PAL. There's no reply and the **BUGS** and **VIRUSES** continue their **ATTACK**! You are helpless ...

DA-DA-DAAAH!
You've been bugged! **Go back to 1.**

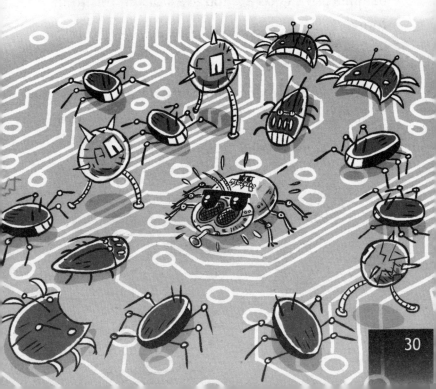

"Turn me into a speedboat," you tell PAL.

The computer obeys and soon you are speeding across the sea.

"Any sign of *MEGABITE*?" you ask.

Before PAL can answer, a huge white shark leaps out of the water and lands on top of you!

You are amazed as it starts to speak.

"Hello! It's me, *MEGABITE*! I can be anything in the virtual world! And I really have got a *MEGA BITE*!"

The shark leaps back into the water, circles around and speeds towards you, jaws open, teeth bared!

To speed away, go to 46.
To change form, go to 8.

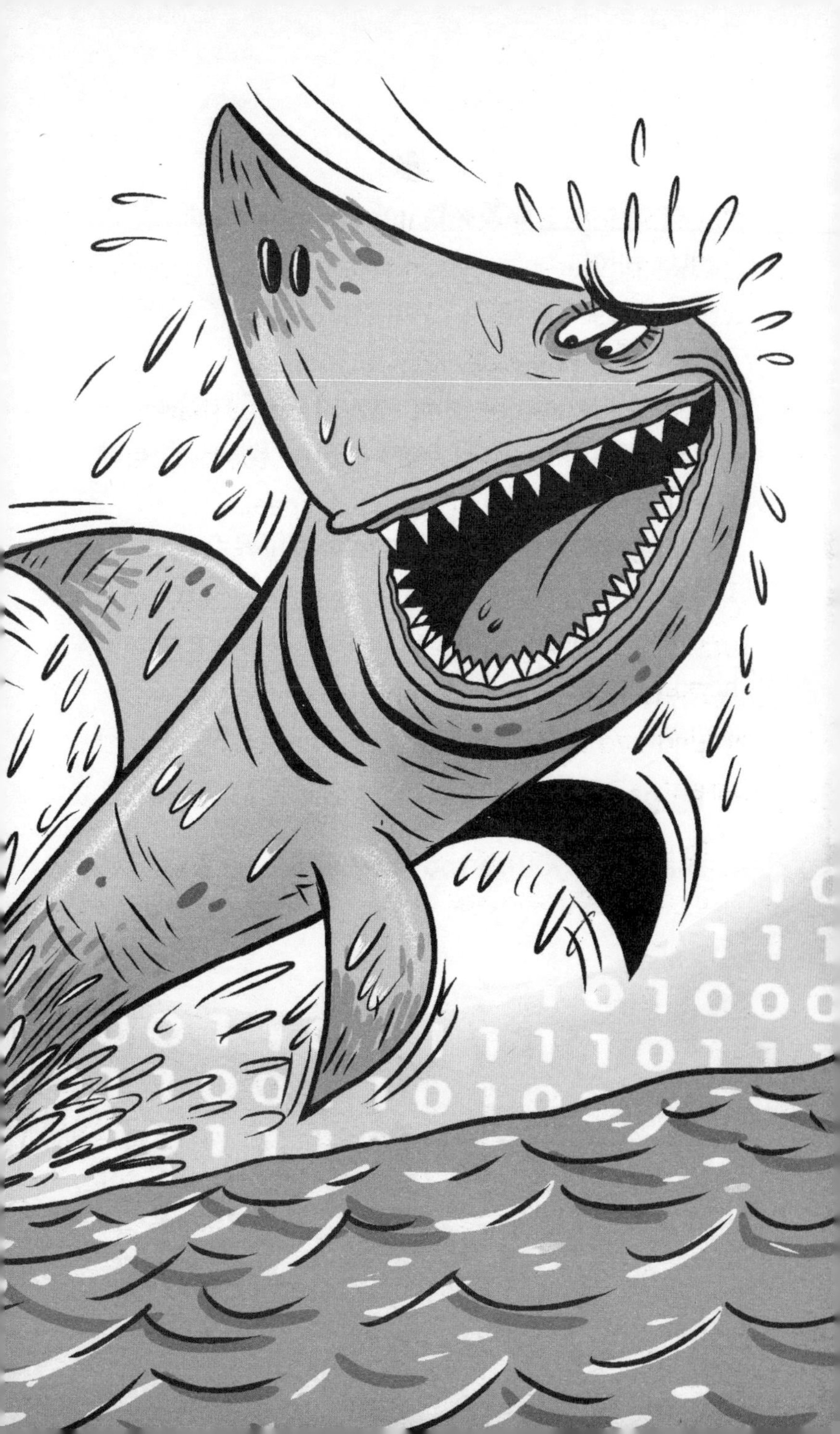

PAL opens up a **COMMS** link to the leader of fighter pilots.

"Stop your attack," you say, "I'm not a **UFO**, I'm *MEGAHERO*!"

"That's what any alien would say," replies the leader. "We don't believe you! Pilots, fire at will."

"My name's not **Will**, I'm *MEGAHERO*! Don't shoot!"

But the pilots ignore you. Dozens more missiles head your way.

"PAL, turn me into a ..."

DA-DA-DAAAH!

Blast it — you're too late! *Go back to 1.*

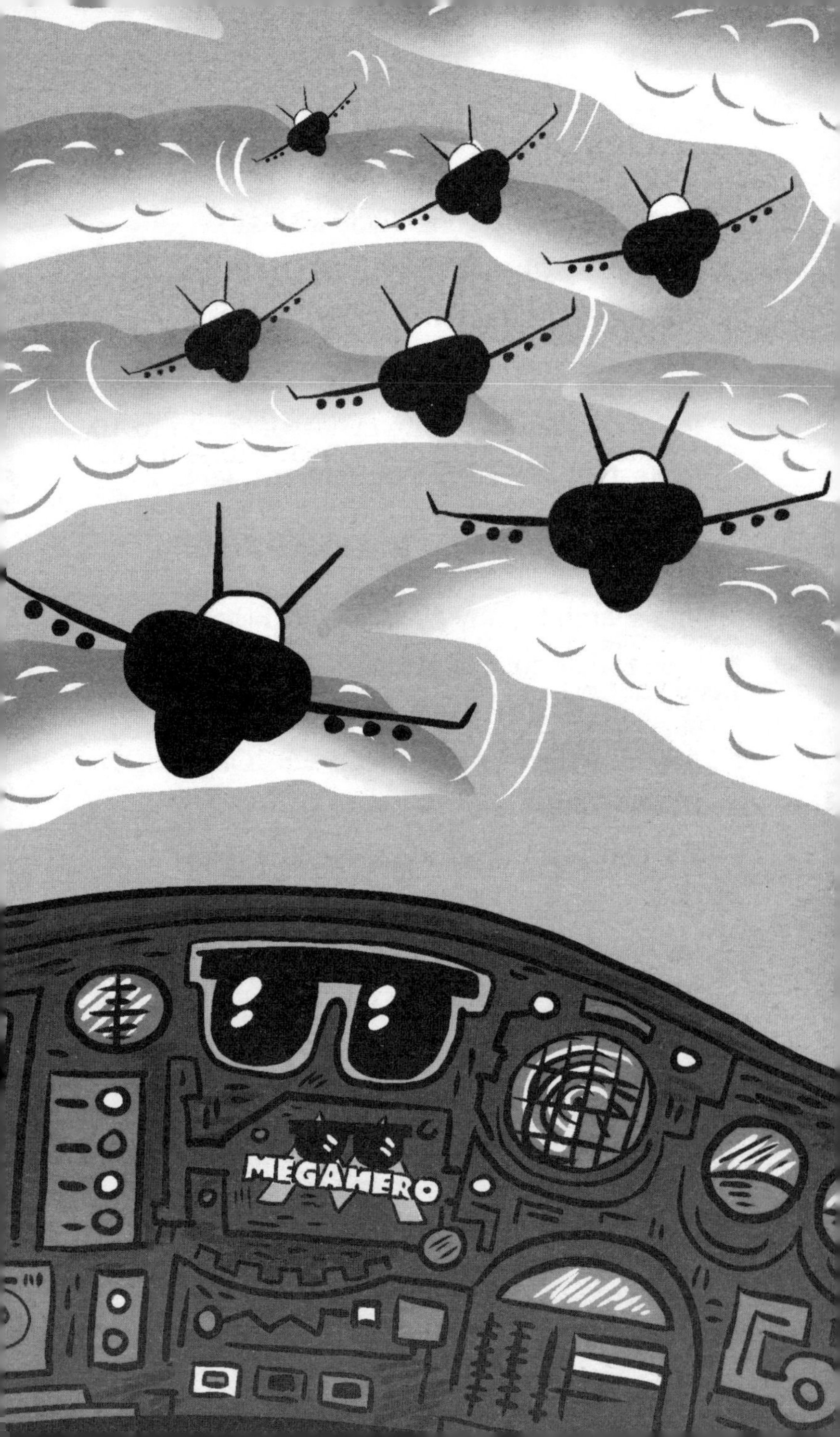
MEGAHERO

33

"Where's **MEGABITE** gone?" you ask PAL.

"HE'S ZAPPED HIMSELF INTO CYBERSPACE! HE COULD GO ANYWHERE AND RESTART HIS WICKED SCHEMES!"

"Then we need to stop him!" you say.

To follow **MEGABITE** into cyberspace, go to 10.

To destroy **MEGABITE**'s equipment, go to 29.

34

"Run a search for any **MEGA VILLAINS** that might be responsible for the attack," you tell PAL. "Start with **SUSHI MAN, THE QUEEN OF HEARTS, MISS TAKE, PROFESSOR WEIRD** and **DINASAW.**"

The computer begins to search the **MEGA VILLAIN** database, when suddenly ...

"**WIBBLE, WOBBLE, FIZZ!**"

"Oh no! Not again!" you cry.

Whoever put the bugs in the system has activated more bugs and viruses! Once again smoke begins to pour out of PAL's circuits.

"**FIZZ 'N' CHIPS**! CUT THE **POWER**," cries PAL. "OR ELSE IT'S THE END FOR US!"

Go to 43.

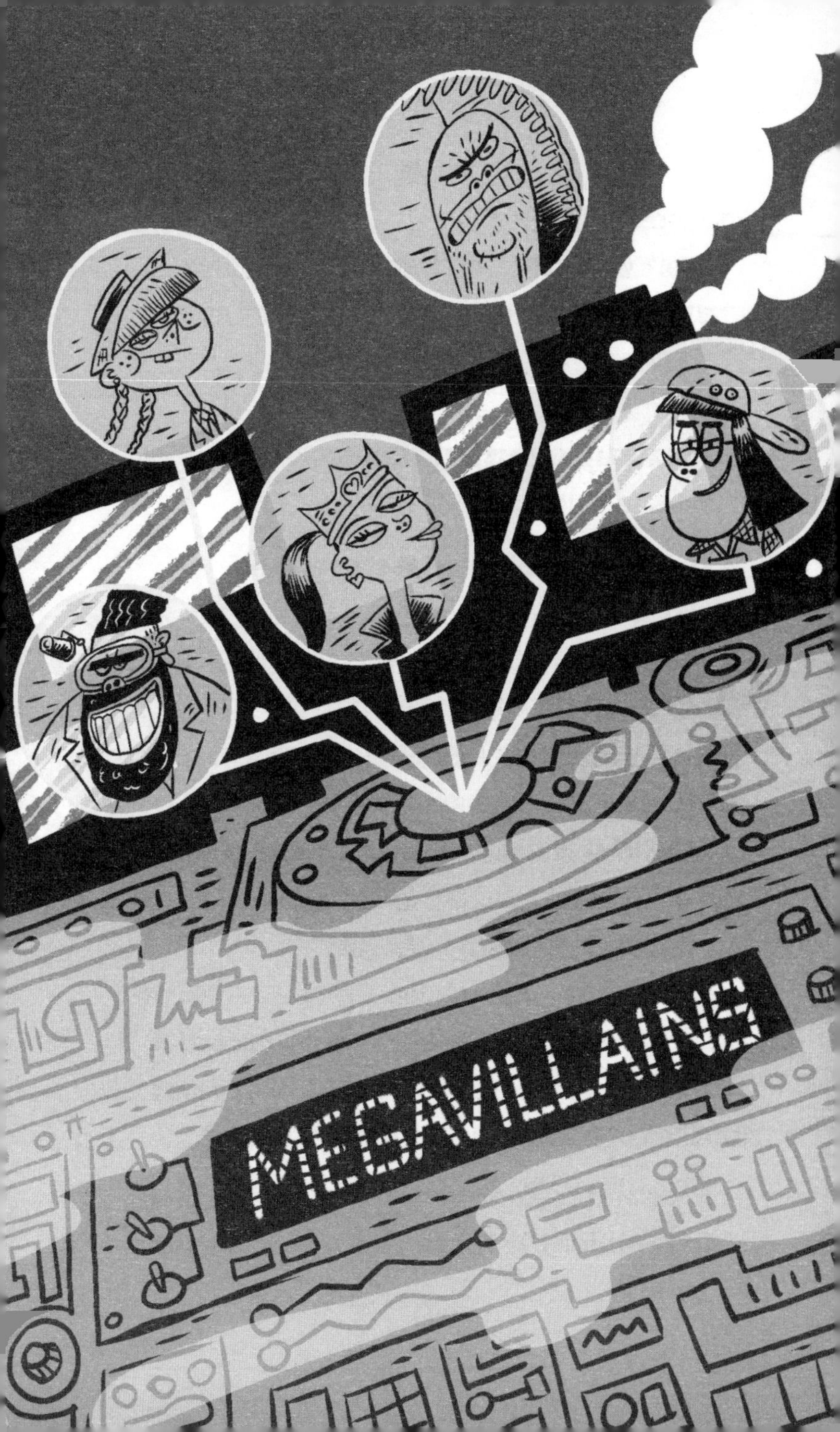
MEGAVILLAINS

35

You press **DELETE**.

"**NO!**" warns PAL. "YOU'RE STILL CONNECTED TO **MEGABITE**'S SYSTEMS – YOU'RE GOING TO DELETE EVERYTHING – INCLUDING **ME**!"

But it's too late.

"**FIZZ! FLIPPITY FIZZ! BUZZ, ZOINK!**"

PAL shuts down **FOREVER**.

That was a *MEGA* mistake to make!
Go back to 1.

36

"Turn me back into a **BUG**!"

PAL obeys and you are back in the cyber world.

"The hacker must be using a system of blockers and re-routers," you tell PAL. "We need to find out this pathway. What you got?"

Minutes later PAL replies. "FOUND IT! THERE WAS A CLOAKING DEVICE. IT WAS HIDING ALL INFORMATION ABOUT THE HACKER. BUT I'VE GOT THROUGH IT. I HAVE THE HACKER'S CO-ORDINATES. THEY ARE IN **LONDON**."

To return to Earth as a spaceship, go to 28.
To head for the hacker through cyberspace, go to 3.

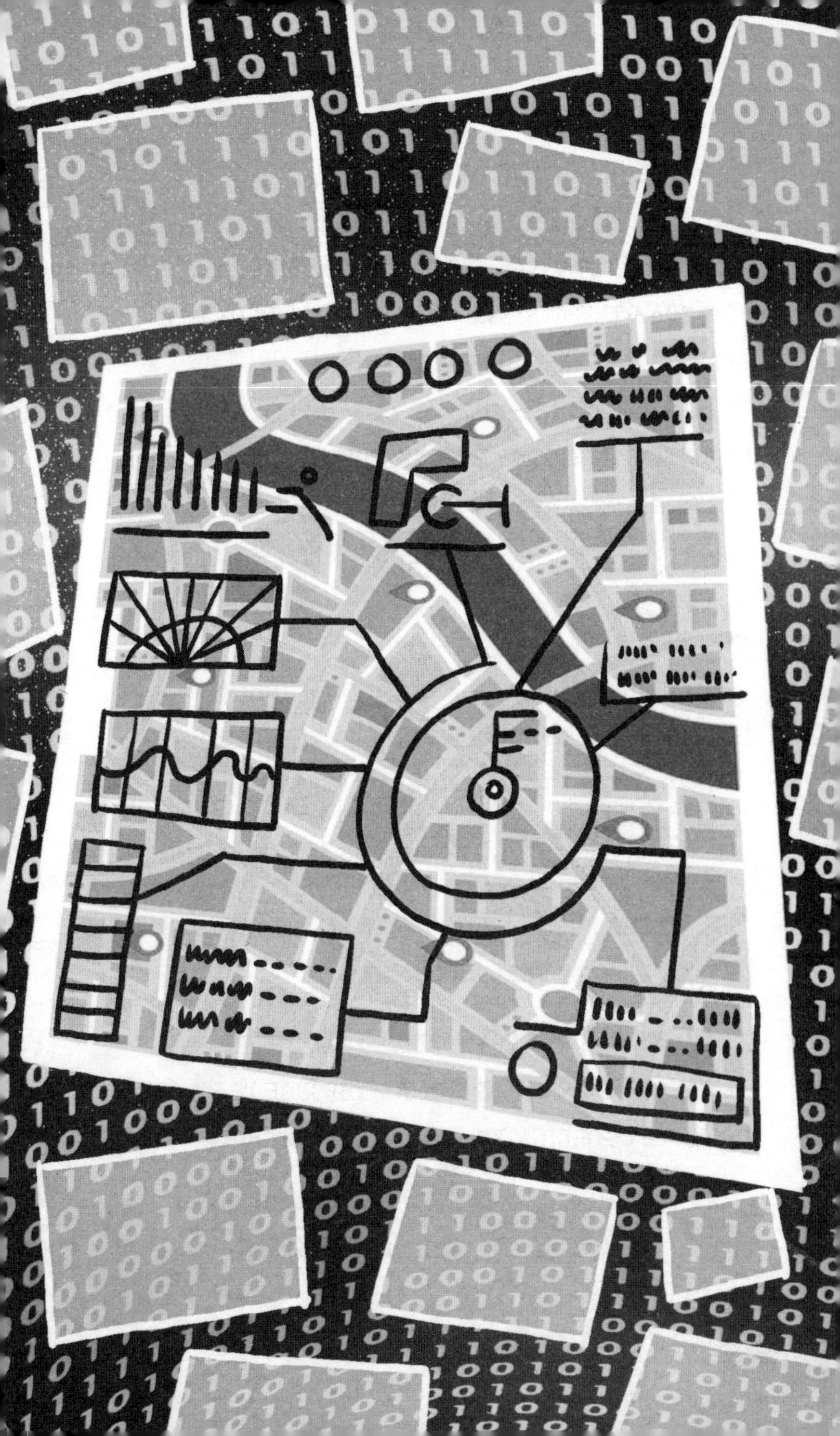

"Let's check out a virtual reality," you tell PAL.

Instantly, your surroundings change. You are in a world of floating bubbles and rainbows. Then, in the blink of an eye, it changes and you find yourself on a small desert island. You are no longer a tracker cookie. You've mysteriously transformed into a giant, sugary biscuit!

"This is weird, I'm a dough cookie!" you say.

"SWEET," replies PAL. "VIRTUAL REALITY IS A **STRANGE** PLACE!"

Suddenly, from out of the sea, emerge thousands of strange-looking buggy creatures.

"What are these sea bugs?" you ask PAL.

"THEY'RE **C-BUGS**!" says PAL

"That's what I said," you reply.

"NOT **SEA BUGS** – THEY'RE **C-BUGS**. C STANDS FOR **CYBER** AND THEY **FEED ON COOKIES**!"

To get out of virtual reality, go to 16.
To change form, go to 21.

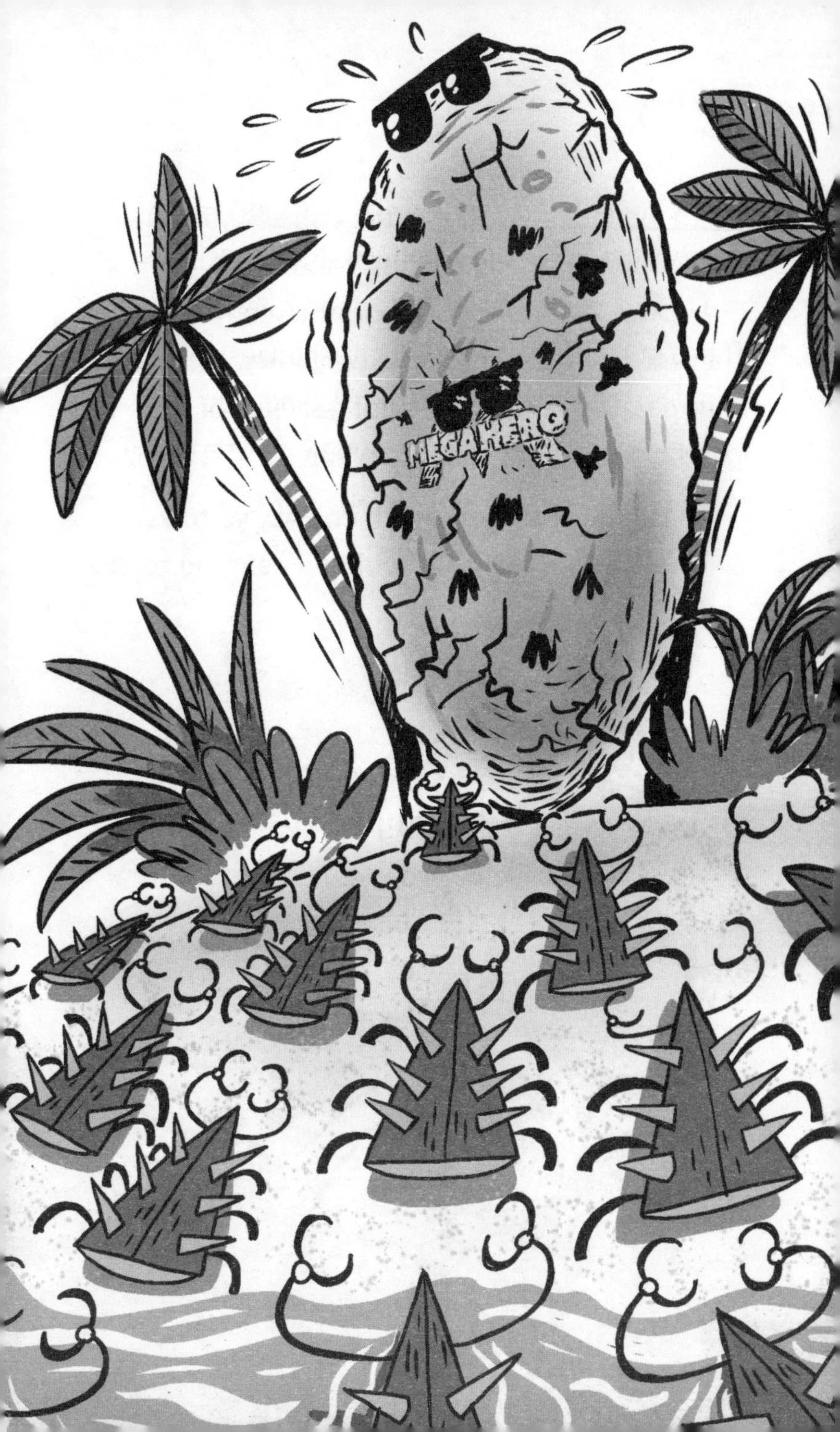
MEGAHERO

"Turn me into a CO_2 fire extinguisher!" you tell PAL, hoping the computer isn't too fried.

Luckily, PAL has enough power to obey and you transform into a giant fire extinguisher. You point your nozzle at PAL and let rip! A stream of CO_2 covers PAL and the flames die out.

To run an antivirus check on PAL, go to 7.

To ask PAL what you should do next, go to 26.

39

"Turn me into a drone," you tell PAL.

You are soon flying across the sea. Time passes, but there is no sign of *MEGABITE*.

"Have you found anything yet?" you ask PAL.

"THERE'S NO TRACE OF HIM AT ALL," replies the computer.

Suddenly an alarm begins to sounds. *BEEP! BEEP!*

"What's the matter?" you ask.

"Your power levels are running low. You can't stay in drone form for much longer in this virtual world."

To change form, go to 31.

To explore the Shadow web, go to 25.

40

"Upload now!" you order PAL. "Firewall off and on!"

The computer obeys and you slip through the firewall before the hacker's **BUGS** and **VIRUSES** can get through it.

To destroy the BUGS and VIRUSES, go to 23.

To track down the hacker, go to 9.

41

"*Surrender!*" you say.

"Never! I can turn into anything in this virtual world!" Proving his claim, *MEGABITE* transforms into a sea monster with lots of tentacles, which grab hold of you and pull you towards its *MEGA* mouth with lots of pointy teeth!

"I think I need to get out of here!" you say.

"**MEGA IDEA!**" PAL replies and transforms you into a *MEGA* computer keyboard.

"What are you doing?"

"TRUST ME, I'M HELPING YOU TO **ESCAPE**!" replies PAL.

To trust PAL, go to 13.
To change into something else, go to 18.

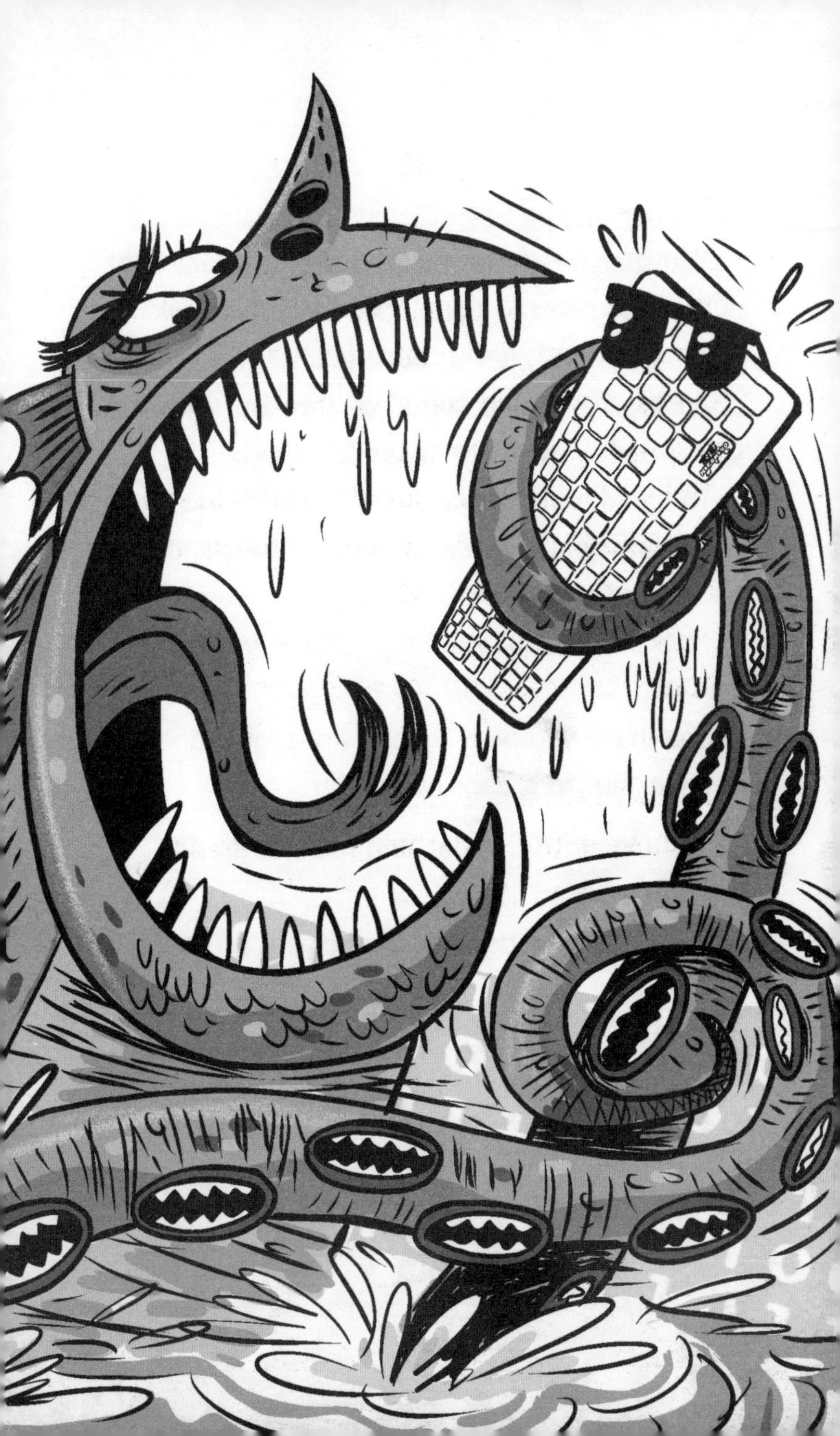

"Turn me into an eagle!" you tell PAL.

You suddenly have a strong desire to eat a lot of fish and poop on people's heads. "Squawk! I said an '**EAGLE**', not a '**SEAGULL**'."

"**OOPS,** SORRY!" PAL turns you into an eagle and you speed away as the fighters zoom by.

PAL guides you towards the hacker's location. Eventually you arrive at a block of flats and turn back into human form.

"THE SOURCE IS ON THE 10TH FLOOR, FLAT 101," says PAL.

You make your way up and are soon standing outside the front door of the flat.

To burst into the flat and make a grand entrance, go to 15.

To sneak into the flat unnoticed, go to 24.

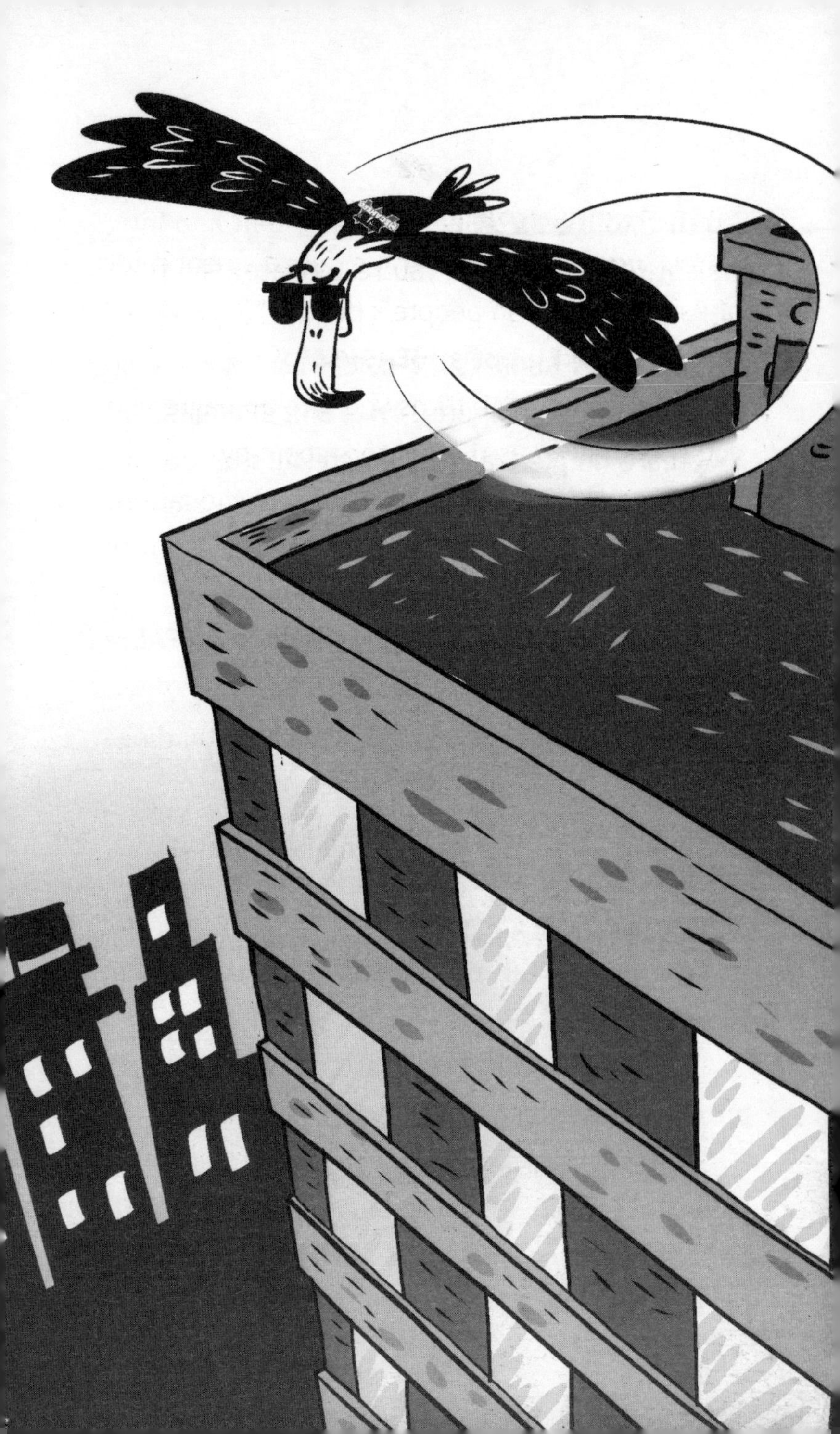

43

You rush to the **MEGA** cave's power unit and hit the cut-off switch. But you're too late, PAL is badly infected.

"TOO MANY BUGS! CAN'T COMPUTE!" More smoke pours from the computer. **"B ... B ... BYEEEEEE ..."**

You are helpless as you watch PAL shut down ... FOREVER!

DA-DA-DAAAH!

You can't be a **MEGAHERO** without your PAL! *Go back to 1.*

44

"I need more pulling power!" you tell PAL.

You transform into an octopus and wrap your arms around the computer.

"You won't beat me, **MEGABITE**!" you say. "I'm too well armed!"

"But I can do this." He starts to tickle your armpits. "I'm going to give you ten tickles!"

"That's a very bad joke," you reply. But nevertheless, you begin to laugh and your hold on the computer weakens as **MEGABITE** continues his ticklish attack.

"PAL, help me," you cry.

"THINK ABOUT YOUR INK!" replies the computer.

"Of course!" you say. You point your bottom at **MEGABITE**.

SPLURT!

You shoot out a jet of black ink. It hits *MEGABITE* in the face and he lets go of the computer.

You turn back into human form. "It's over, *MEGABITE*, or rather, *MEGA LIGHTWEIGHT*!"

MEGABITE wipes the ink from his face. "I don't think so! I still have voice control over the computer. See you later, suckers. **ENTER!**"

There is a burst of light and *MEGABITE* disappears!

Go to 33.

45

"Set up a firewall so the **BUGS** and **VIRUSES** can't get into your system again. And I don't mean a real **WALL OF FIRE!**"

"AS IF I'D BE THAT STUPID," replies PAL, in a hurt voice. "ELECTRONIC FIREWALL SET."

"Open up the website," you order.

IMMEDIATELY millions of **BUGS** and **VIRUSES** invade PAL's systems. They smash against the **FIREWALL**, fighting to get through.

To destroy the BUGS and VIRUSES, go to 23.

To sneak through the firewall to get to the hacker, go to 11.

You increase speed, but **MEGABITE** closes in on you. Its deadly jaws open, revealing rows of razor sharp teeth.

"It's closing in on my bottom!" you tell PAL.

SNAP!

MEGABITE's jaws shut tight, just missing you!

"That was close, PAL!" you shout. "My stern nearly had a **MEGABITE**!"

But there's no time to relax. **MEGABITE** attacks once more.

SNAP!

Again, your bottom manages to escape a toothy bite!

"This is only going to end one way," you tell PAL. "We need to do something before my back end is ended!"

To change into a bird, go to 18.
To change into a bigger boat, go to 8.

"Turn me into a spaceship before I run out of breath!" you order PAL.

PAL obeys but you find yourself floating away from the satellite. You look down and see you have a woolly coat, four hooves and a space helmet!

"I said a **SPACESHIP** not a **SPACE SHEEP**! Get me **BAAAAAAAACK** before my breath runs out and ..."

DA-DA-DAAAH!

Too late! *Go back to 1.*

48

"Before we do anything else, we need to debug you," you tell PAL. "Run a **MEGA** scan and quarantine any bad stuff. We don't want you going up in smoke again!"

Minutes later PAL is back up and running normally.

"ALL BUGS AND VIRUSES ARE QUARANTINED. I MUST SAY, I'M FEELING A LOT BETTER."

"Now we need to find out who is responsible for this," you say.

To search your **MEGA VILLAIN** database for clues, go to 4.

To set a trap for the hacker, go to 20.

49

As you step forward, *MEGABITE* hits his keyboard.

You suddenly feel yourself transforming. You have become a baby!

"PAL, what are you doing?" you gurgle.

"Nothing!" replies *MEGABITE*. "You walked or rather, smashed your way into my trap! I've taken over your **COMMS** link to PAL. I control you now! And with you out of the way, I can begin my **WORLD DOMINATION PLAN!**"

He hits the keyboard again, turning you into a plastic duck! "Oh, I love this," cries *MEGABITE*. "I can turn you into **ANYTHING I WANT, FOREVER!**"

DA-DA-DAAAH!

Things have taken a turn for the worse!
Go back to 1.

50

"With *MEGABITE* in quarantine, the Internet is safe once more," you tell PAL. "I think it's time for a holiday."

"WHAT ABOUT THOSE NEW PANTS YOU WANTED TO BUY?" says PAL.

"I'll give them a miss. I'm going to Hawaii and you can turn me into a surfboard. That's the only bit of surfing I'm going to be doing for a while!"

The End!

THE HATEFUL HORRORS OF THE
QUEEN OF HEARTS

Steve Barlow · Steve Skidmore
Illustrated by Pipi Sposito

You are in the *MEGA* cave playing a game of cards with PAL.

You lay down the KING OF SPADES.

"SNAP!" says PAL.

"But you haven't even played your card yet!" you protest.

The KING OF SPADES appears on PAL's holographic screen.

"How did you know?" you ask.

"I CAN PREDICT WHAT'S COMING NEXT," says PAL, smugly.

Suddenly the *MEGA ALARM* rings out.

"*CRIME ALERT! CRIME ALERT!*"

"You didn't predict that," you say.

"IT'S PROBABLY NOT IMPORTANT!" replies PAL.

To see what the crime is, go to 24.
To carry on playing cards, go to 48.

CONTINUE THE ADVENTURE IN:

THE HATEFUL HORRORS OF THE
QUEEN OF HEARTS

About the 2Steves

"The 2Steves" are
Britain's most popular
writing double act for
young people, specialising
in comedy and adventure.
They perform regularly in
schools and libraries, and at festivals, taking the
power of words and story to audiences of all ages.

Together they have written many books, including the
I HERO Immortals and *I HERO Toons* series.

About the illustrator:
Pipi Sposito

Pipi was born in Buenos Aires in
the fabulous 60's and has always
drawn. As a little child, he used
to make modelling clay figures, too.
At the age of 19 he found out
he could earn a living by drawing. He now develops
cartoons and children's illustrations in different
artistic styles, and also 3D figures, puppets and
caricatures. Pipi always listens to music when he works.

Have you completed these I HERO adventures?

I HERO Immortals — more to enjoy!

Dinosaur Hunter

Steve Barlow – Steve Skidmore
Illustrated by Jack Lawrence

978 1 4451 6963 7 pb
978 1 4451 6964 4 ebook

Fairy

Steve Barlow – Steve Skidmore
Illustrated by Jack Lawrence

978 1 4451 6969 9 pb
978 1 4451 6971 2 ebook

Knight

Steve Barlow – Steve Skidmore
Illustrated by Jack Lawrence

978 1 4451 6957 6 pb
978 1 4451 6959 0 ebook

Pirate Queen

Steve Barlow – Steve Skidmore
Illustrated by Jack Lawrence

978 1 4451 6954 5 pb
978 1 4451 6955 2 ebook

Samurai

Steve Barlow – Steve Skidmore
Illustrated by Jack Lawrence

978 1 4451 6960 6 pb
978 1 4451 6962 0 ebook

Witch

Steve Barlow – Steve Skidmore
Illustrated by Jack Lawrence

978 1 4451 6966 8 pb
978 1 4451 6967 5 ebook

Defeat all the baddies in Toons:

KILLER CUSTARD

Steve Barlow • Steve Skidmore

978 1 4451 5930 0 pb
978 1 4451 5931 7 ebook

ROBIN HAMSTER

Steve Barlow • Steve Skidmore

978 1 4451 5921 8 pb
978 1 4451 5922 5 ebook

ENTER the PENGUIN

Steve Barlow • Steve Skidmore

978 1 4451 5924 9 pb
978 1 4451 5925 6 ebook

KUNG FU KITTEN

Steve Barlow • Steve Skidmore

978 1 4451 5918 8 pb
978 1 4451 5919 5 ebook

Also by the 2Steves...

GALAXY FOOTBALL CUP

978 1 4451 5985 0 hb
978 1 4451 5986 7 pb

MOVIE STAR SET-UP

978 1 4451 5976 8 hb
978 14451 5977 5 pb

ROBOT RAMPAGE

978 1 4451 5982 9 hb
978 1 4451 5983 6 pb

SMALL WORLD

978 1 4451 5972 0 hb
978 1 4451 5971 3 pb

SPACE CHASE

978 1 4451 5892 1 hb
978 1 4451 5891 4 pb

SPACE PIRATES

978 1 4451 5988 1 hb
9781 4451 5989 8 pb

SPACE RAP

978 1 4451 5973 7 hb
978 1 4451 5974 4 pb

WEB WORLD

978 1 4451 5979 9 hb
978 1 4451 5980 5 pb